GETTING OVER
Mr Zane –
STEPPING OUT

GETTING OVER *Mr Zane -* STEPPING OUT

HARRY STEFANO

ISBN: 978-1-63684-595-1   (PB)
ISBN: 978-1-63684-596-8   (HB)
ISBN: 978-1-63684-594-4   (E-book)

Some characters and events in this book are fictitious and products of the author's imagination. Any similarity to real persons, living or dead, is coincidental and not intended by the author.

The Universal Pages
Bryant Park 510, Fifth Avenue Floor 3
New York, NY 10036, USA

press@theuniversalpages.com
www.theuniversalpages.com

Printed in the United States of America

Introduction

Already I have noticed a good difference since not having my depot injection as I felt more able to walk- and not so much an effort. Weighed at 15stone 13lbs!!! Hopefully things should improve, but little step by step- I hope that within the month I should make it back to some form of regular physical exercise- this should be assisted by less sedative drugs being left in my system- when I consider how active I have been in the past it's hard to believe the figure I have now. Which is what prompted me to take such what could be viewed as drastic action by refusing my depot injection. The way I see it I'm 27 years old and a size 20 in clothes; I don't want to be this size- so it was really a simple choice for me- I need more not less energy to be able to function and enjoy the exercise/classes I used to (when I tell you of how daunting an experience it will be to go back to them to face the people there......)- and dress more trendy; instead of looking and feeling like and old woman (with next to no energy levels and sleeping all the time).This is what adds to my depression- and therefore worsens my condition (the more I think about my body image the more depressed I feel- to the point of tears; when I think of all the work I'd done previously and how physically fit I was). This is why today I daren't dwell on it- and I have to whilst remaining realistic; I have to be positive therefore in around a month's time (when hopefully my energy levels are a little better e.g. higher I'm going to do something constructive and along with exercise put myself on a strict diet)

Well here I am again, on a new voyage and at the start of rebuilding my life again. One thing I have come to notice is that only I can change the future and prepare myself for a life of happiness and fulfilment. I think what will make these changes possible and what will make me happy? These are things I have gone through life not really knowing up until now at this precise moment I have to consider and contemplate these important things. I feel very strongly that if I have love in my life then this will greatly improve my quality of life. But I have come to realise that I have placed too great a deal in this indescribable love aspect; so if I don't know what it is, how am I ever to achieve this? I have come to realise that I have placed too much a higher power in searching for love in all the wrong places, looking to find love with and from other people, all of which have let me down in some way or another. But I have had a glimpse of love and found none truer and more fulfilling than the love I found in myself, I had a glimpse of this last year, but it was short lived. I wish I could regain this, I know I can regain this love of myself again, but it takes time, and I am beginning to accept and learn again how to love myself. It's a painfully slow process, but I believe in myself, through all my ups and downs and life's troubles I have always somehow retained a very strong belief in myself, almost a stubbornness that won't give in, something which I can't ignore, and I must be true to this always. I have been diagnosed with borderline manic depression for almost four years now, it's not something which I readily comply with in terms of acceptance, cos then it's like admitting that I have an illness a disease and for the most part something which everyone else seems to be afraid of; all accept me. I am in denial still, illness reeks of unspeakable connotations, and is not something which I am prepared to foster, so I chose not to take medication. Recovery is a process of which progress can be frustratingly slow. I am experimenting with a new perspective on this occasion, one which involves group therapy, as well as incorporating religion. I am more mindful of my condition, and have come to realise that I must treat myself with more care firstly mentally. I have come to realise the importance of looking after your head as it were, and as scary as it sounds I know I have issues, issues that I have left unresolved for years, not facing up to myself, allowing myself to run wild as it were, even at times without a care in for other people. I think I have always had behavioural problems, coming from a nervous disposition early on, I had the less than idealic childhood. Sometimes I'm still a child that never quite matured in the proper way that other people did. I think my key word today has to be 'control', being 'in control' of myself. This is where I take responsibility for admitting that my behaviour has become unmanageable and out of control, this is step one of the NA programme, I have wormed my way in my leaning on an addiction to food, even so NA can still help me on so many levels. They provide some good advice that helps me in this emotional behavioural way. I have the potential to be counselled, but I'm too scared, it all sounds quite confrontational, and I don't think that it's fare to place all my burdens on food, which would form the basis of my counselling sessions. Therefore am I going back on my initial thoughts that I am a food addict? Trying to justify and talk my way out of it, as usual? Maybe I am, therefore it is an issue. As part of loving myself I have to be honest and say that food had become quite a significant part of my life at the moment. Then another piece of NA advice is to take one day at a time, and not letting one bad day ruin my week. I can certainly see how food did play a very heavy role in the past few months, but today I have to say that it was not that bad in comparison to then. Food was my friend my comfort, unquestioning and always there. But now today I feel that its` grip is loosening slightly, food no longer has the great appeal it did. I can notice this by how I don't gauge myself to the point of nausea trying to finish every last mouthful on my plate; I now know that it's ok to leave what I don't want to eat cos feel full. I never thought I'd be able to actually 'feel full' again. It's almost can be likened to a cognitive behaviour, and learning all over again to eat in a healthy way, and to be in control. I feel like I am beginning to regain some self-control around food again. And as simple as it sounds I am not starving myself but instead eating when I am hungry, as simple advice as it seems, it has proven to be the most effective yet in breaking this vicious cycle of overeating. I have learned how to eat when I am hungry by consciously asking myself am I hungry, or am I trying to change the way I feel? This to me has indicated great progress mentally, if not physically, but not to be too hard on myself as I haven't creeped back over the 15 stone mark on the scales. It's all about addressing the mind-body balance, and I feel that my mind is starting to get healthier, and to me that's progress, real progress! I ate what I wanted also but I just have to work on the 'enjoying every mouthful' bit cos I did cheat on this, especially with the awful cheese I ate, I should have left it cos it was gross. But I did leave a good portion of food on my dinner plate as well as only eating and enjoying almost half of my cheesecake. But never mind, cos I can restart afresh tomorrow, and I hope that in time I can retune my faults of yesterday and start again. Starting again is a wonderful thing in this respect, cos everything's a blank canvas, except when you realise how you're correcting yourself and there are many and tiring list of alterations to be made; but this is all part of my progress.

I now have to look outside from food, and as the boredom rears its welcomed head, I have to address a new way of life for myself. So in one thought I have to answer that 'yes I am an addict, cos I've lived to use food and used food to live' and when I take away this there's nothing left, this is how empty my life has become, the only indication of this being boredom itself, highlighting to me once again how my life is far from perfect, and how my life has become unmanageable. And so as I'm told in NA to keep coming back.

Everybody wants answers, solutions to their life's problems, of which there are no clear-cut and dried ones, and certainly what may be right for one person may not suit another. But I think that the first step in the right direction is considering that I want to change my life for the better, and how I go about this remains to be seen in an extraordinary way, I think this comes back to progress, and it being a slow process. I have accepted now not to be too hard on myself, cos I had a lot of demands made on me from early on, and always pushing myself too hard, to a level that was not sustainable, and then another relapse. So I have not placed any great demands on myself at the moment, and instead have decided not to fight against my natural recovery rate however long it might take. I know I will get there in time. I know that in the past I hadn't fully recovered, and I have taken many shortcuts at my own risk. This I realise that I certainly missed the mental aspect of it, yet it was my emotional sanity that I gave least regard for, very selfishly and foolishly this was the very thing which suffered more and more every time. Now though I am listening to my emotions more, and I am starting to live a healthier life. I felt good to go for a cycle tonight, it may have been dark, but I felt the urge to do this, and so indulged myself cos exercise is something which I had been struggling with trying to motivate myself, and it felt good, just losing myself in my music as I cycled. No worries and no problems, just a clear head and focussing on the road ahead. Just for today...

Well I attended my NA meeting this evening, a real achievement to actually go! I always feel a sense of trying to get out of going, and I think if it wasn't for prompting I would surely be happy to miss out altogether. Which is a sad reflection when I think of how I should be going for my own ends primarily, when instead I'm left thinking of how I'll letting anyone down. Surely I owe it to myself to be there more than ever. I have come to realise and accept a sense of belonging there, amongst those who have lost their way on life's` path, and somehow have made it back from the brink of self-destruction. I really have learned so much, and am gaining new knowledge and insight all the time into my condition and illness. I have come to know that I need to be there, even thought I am still yet to speak and to share openly with others. When I think of how my mindset was previously in terms of how I once associated druggies and such with being losers and wastes of space, only to find myself in the exact same category, I thought that I was above them, and yet in their presence I feel so humbled. I admire their bravery to be honest and open with others; as I struggle to find the words to express what I'm feeling, but when I stop to think about this I find that I am lost for words and my whole vocabulary as eloquently as I once presumed is greatly lacking. I have become introvert, perhaps, but then I feel nothing, almost a sense of numbness clinging to the memories of the past, these are what keep me company on the lonely nights I spend in remembering. I have discovered that I live too much in the past, and can spend hours pondering the great what was. But this is smudged my how if it was that great then I would still be living in those times, and then I come to realise how those memories were not at all the great times that I so readily remember. Yes I had good times, and bad. But even the good times were a lie, but yes I had good times; but life goes on, and things change life happens an ideal situation remains so and is forever encapsulated in that perfect moment. Perfectionism is something which is not real, something that could be solidly set in cement unchanging through time would be forever bliss. I have placed too high a price on my past memories, cos this is all that it is now a space in time a place in time where I once lived, I cannot go on existing in the present through recungering memories from the past, trying to relive it in parts that I chose. There are no dress rehearsals not to sound to cliché as in order to relive the past you need someone else to play a part, is fantasy a better way of coping with reality. Yes it is escapism, escaping from life, reality, cos I hate it so much my existence, the grimness of it all, and I have to face up to being unhappy. Instead of whaling and crying, I remain composed and almost cold with emotion. I think it is all very sobering. But I am facing my fears I suppose I am learning to come to terms with my problems and address them head on. I am journeying with a group of other people, all of which are quality individuals, its funny how you can have so much in common with the very people who you once detested and scorned. The people who I would once pass and cross over onto the other side of the street, thinking I was better than that. Perhaps this is why I have come to remain so quiet during meetings, because then I will have to admit how I am just as human as they are, and dare I say how I need their help, and their support, I need their friendship, their approval and acceptance. Perhaps it's part of me admitting how I'm normal, not extraordinary but plain and ordinary, I think I feared how they would see through my façade and bullshit that I have all through my life done. Everything in neat little packages bundled away and out of sight cos the thought of looking would shock me, even though I know the truth really deep down. Or do I? For the first time in my life I'm being honest with myself and it scares me to death. My new key word today is acceptance, of myself. I can no longer boast and play the proud ambitious high flyer, an image that I would always resort to portraying, instead of now when I realise that how when it's all stripped away I am left with a shell. What happened to the confident outgoing go-getter? Where has she gone now, my illness has killed her. I am left looking at a person I no longer recognise in the mirror with a behavioural mannerism that is alien to me. I am fragile and feel as though I am stripped naked for the world to look at. And I did not like what I saw when faced with the reality. If I was talking to one of my old school friends now they might remark how sad alive I have, and what happened to harry? But even then I have come to realise that I was trying to be someone else cos I didn't like myself. I have come to realise how did I ever really know myself? Do other people have an insight into me that perhaps could argue they know me better than I know myself. So I have to really find out who I am, amidst the masks of the past and the various other ways I tried to escape from life through drink, nicotine and always my old friend ever dependable food.

So here I am doing it again beating myself up, I'm good at that, putting myself down. Cos my father used to beat me, now I seem to have taken over that role of knowing just how to make myself feel shitty. I have to stop this unhealthy mental torture, and so I tell myself to let it go, it wasn't nor was it ever my fault, I am not to blame, I am the victim, I correct I was the victim, I survived, as so many other people do. When I would push myself in nearly all aspects of my life in an overwhelming desire to control everything I have to stop and say that I never enjoyed asking the superhuman of myself, and it's no wonder every time I have a breakdown. I have to stop punishing myself. Which is why I suppose I so hold on to the one love that I knew, cos nobody ever loved me like that before. And now I have to face up to being truthful and honest with myself and I have to let him go. I even have to question the extent of this love, cos if I was talking to my Nan she would say the same of do you think it is love to treat someone in this way. Again part of a pattern, in terms of a destructive relationship with my dad and most other boyfriends afterwards. Because he treated me badly I loved him more for this, I thought it was love, love doesn't hurt so much and therefore that's how you know that you love someone. That's a sick and twisted version of the truth. Have to see it for what it was, a very emotional time, a time of guilt, anxiety, and even though I was with him a longing for him never to leave me. This ghost is something which has been an issue for years, and I knew that one day I would have to face head-on and admit the truth, I have to do this now, now that I feel strong enough to take this on and win this time. I have to say goodbye to him, I have to stop ploughing money that I can't afford on indulging in psychics to tell me mumbo jumbo, as this is not helping me, and instead it is fuelling falseness, and lies. I cannot believe how I have been wittingly lying to myself, and I seek comfort in these lies. I have invested foolishly hundreds of pounds in fantasy, just so long as they say all the right words, if not I find someone else who will tell me what I want to hear, and spend even greater amounts of money, as a quick fix out of the reality of the situation. I know that if my Nan was here now she would tell me to belt up, and not to waste any more of my life on this man who had brought me nothing but pain, he will never make me happy. How foolish I was to console myself that he should wish to keep me his mistress entrapped within the confines of the mental health system cos then I would remain forever hopeless and drugged and fat and alone, with no prospects, now I see how he will win if I continue to foster such deluded ideas and if I do not let him go he will continue to destroy me. I used to think how he was the best by far and I really admired him. I have only ever confided this in my Aunt, and she believed me, so I no longer and have learned not to discuss this with anyone else cos they would think I was crazy, for when I described this a little to another at one time he quite rightly remarked of how, "well it sounds to me as though this guy is a prick". It's funny how something so crude can hit all the right nails on the head, and is probably the most sensible thing I have ever heard on this subject. How true he was, this coming from anther man, I half expected in anticipation that he might side with his fellow male counterpart, but he did him no favours, I thought that he may have said something more encouraging if only to help me understand him, still trying to find excuses for his behaviour. Although I didn't at the time, I know have come to realise what a great favour he did me. While my Aunt instead indulged me, in the long term it turned out to be the wrong thing to do, cos it turned out to be all quite wrong, he was wrong, and I was wrong to continue to hold onto false hope and lies, she in fact helped to continue this long running issue, as it has been many years that I have kept up the pretence. My Nan would tell me to forget about him, and just suppose I explore this avenue one last time, and things had gone slightly different, just that he was with me, would he actually be with me? I would be a whole lot worse cos he would actually make me unhappy, never mind the havoc that his ghost has made for me, driving me out of my mind, thinking I was madly in love with him, he has done enough damage from a distance. And as Nan would say do you suppose he loses ay sleep over you? He's not a real man if he can stand by and watch the love of his life be alone, this is a man with no backbone, spineless. Despite all the thoughts I used to have of him being a real masculine man; this is a coward. Would I want him now after al this? No I would not, cos as I said to him once you haven't got the balls; and by golly I was right. He even lied about it, to save his own skin, cos he hasn't the balls to admit the truth, someone who would let others think I was deluded and crazy rather than admit the truth, is that someone I want to be with? I don't think so he is totally spineless and he surely doesn't respect me. That is the true measure of himself, after I placed him high up on a pedestal, when I'm honest he amounts to nothing special at all, and yet I want him so much? Oh some sobering thoughts tonight! He's not good enough for me, why would I want to be with someone that made me feel like shit. Someone who has to have his father but him a house cos even he's pretending to be someone he's not cos if he's honest he doesn't like himself, and so changes this cos he can't face reality. At least I face up to how I can give myself credit I am nothing more than what I seem, I no longer feel the need to pretend to be something I'm not, all the money and material aspects in the world will not make me happy and when I had more I never was happy. But I can always say how no one has given me a break in life, everything I take full responsibility for, and I provide for myself, I look after myself. It feels good to be sober and say how I'm in charge here, I look after myself. It feels so good to be regaining and appreciating my independence. I have started to be more responsible with taking proper care of myself, washing and budgeting. And it feels good to no longer feel the need to be dependant on an invisible man, why should I care what he thinks or feels about me, when he clearly doesn't harbour the same concerns for me. He crazily talked of how I would not like what he would do next when I returned home, and he spoke of how he was keen for me to return home where he could keep an eye on me better, as he said how this time he would embed me so far into the mental health system that I would not be able to run away again and escape his grip, his control. This is not love why should I deteste my mother remaining with my controlling father, in an abusive destructive relationship, when I am condoning and glamorising how he really loves me see cos he's never around but treats me like an object, something he owns, like a piece of property. He said as much when he said how you will not leave me, I won't let you, and you are mine. Even though he's never around still his presence is felt everyday when I let him entertain my thoughts, and by my surroundings being the nature that the are, living with crazy people! Yes my Nan would certainly not like him, like the same way she never liked my father, and as she once said how jealousy is not love. I suppose I know I did right when I escaped his family. And the way I can positively remove him forever from my life is to refrain from thinking about him, and perhaps more effectively to never mention him again, and to think about forming new meaningful relationships in the future. I am ready now to love someone else, someone new and be totally committed to them, and them alone, he will not spoil my future happiness, he will no longer control my life, I escaped one monster, and I can escape this monster too!

I feel so much lighter now, and I think I will sleep a little better in my bed, like last night, I had such a well rested sleep, I am surprised at how effective this journal is, and it seems to be helping me in my recovery, I wish I had tried it sooner; it's been so nice to put aside some me time, and be comfortable and even look forward to the prospect of being alone with myself. Things are becoming clearer, I am working through my issues and facing my biggest fear-myself. I have come to liken this journal as almost a means of talking to myself, I remember as a small child I always had a lot on my mind and would spend hour alone talking to myself before falling asleep, I had to get it off my chest, and although sometimes I find it difficult to share with other people it's good to know that I still have a good and true friend in myself especially when writing this journal, cos gone are he days when I could talk to myself and people not suppose that I was crazy! And I think I'd only disturb others in the house, so on a practical level it's a very good tool for helping me to talk through my thought process at this particular time. It's good to become reacquainted with myself, I almost forgot how good and capable I am as a friend and how even if I am in company or no company at all I can always chat with myself like this and I see how responsible and once again how independent I am. I did always like the sound of my own voice in conversations, which is why I am a little worn out now in everyday life situations cos I have no deep and burning desires, as I've addressed them all the night before, and so have reached a nice level of contentment, and not feeling the need to speak all of the time for most of the time; I have become very well used to listening instead and preferring to do this on many occasions now. I think I am becoming a better person for this in terms of becoming more mentally balanced. It's ok to relax, I have nothing to prove, and I am moving along at my own pace...

Today I am so relieved and feel so willing to be alone with myself tonight, I feel like I'm at the start of establishing a deep and meaningful relationship with myself. And I'm starting to like being me. I decided to treat myself and look after myself, I embarked on some rather nice quality purchases. I bought a nice new coat, and a nice pair of cords and a new pair of boots and a nice new cardigan. On one outfit I spent a cool £200. But I know I will get immense pleasure from wearing them. It` s good to take care of myself like this... I deserve it, after all no one else is going to treat me in this way that I deserve to be treated in. It's a nice feeling to get back some of my pride, and to start once more to care about the way I look, my whole appearance. Tonight for the first time in a while I started to recall Francesca whom I was fond of very much. She was a girl who really knew her own mind, and was not afraid to look after herself. She kitted herself out in all the best clothes from top to toe, right down to skin deep, I learned a lot from her, including how to take care of my old friend personal hygiene, I learned how effective it was to use talcum powder and to use perfume and scented moisturiser, I was the essence of Christian Dior, I reeked of it, and I was absolutely in love with the scent. It was a very sophisticated perfume, and I knew that I attracted many male admirers from wearing it, it oozed class and sophistication. Yes this is who I am a lady. I like being well groomed, and my former job enabled me to indulge myself in being well dressed and fashionably so also. I remember recalling how almost all my clothes would tally at a cost of a little over £100 pounds sometimes more. And I felt good. It brought back fond memories to find myself back in Burtons similar to how I did this in Guernsey buying men's jeans cos they were cheaper stylish and still looked good and fit me well. It feels good to be in this space at the moment, and I have taken to not people pleasing so much especially in how I find myself in my room now by choosing to walk away from what appears to be Ians' craziness. As part of my preservation I can't cope with that, I don't want to let anyone interfere with my recovery in a damaging way as to pose a real risk of getting too involved with someone who is showing signs of being unwell. It scares me. And so I applaud myself in realising how this is not my responsibility nor is it my job to interfere in this tricky situation. I think that he has cottoned onto how I am not taking medication, and I have denied it as I don't wish to tell him, simple as that, I don't want to justify it, it's just like that. He's the wrong person to confide in. Especially with his stupid suggestions lately of running off to London and tonight how he asked if we could commit suicide together, it's just insane. But these are his issues not mine. I don't have any thoughts of reckless behaviour or desires to run away, kill myself etc, I am regaining my happiness. Oh Francesca, we were inseparable, and formed a close attachment; I will always remember how strikingly beautiful she is, and how she taught me that I can be a beautiful person too. Which is why I have to keep a check on myself tonight, to keep me stable, I can still be nice, and not get caught up in it, I have done well today. When I recall how I had a good meeting with Nadia, and went off to town, then came home did laundry and ate, and watched TV and had a shower. Then Ian`s nonsense started he said how he hasn't taken his tablets for 2 days now and as a result he is talking all of the time... that just raised a red flag for me and so I made my excuses and left him to it, how sensible I have been. I'm glad that mum was pleased with me today it was good to talk to her, and she also acknowledges my progress; it's good that she would be honest with me if the time arose that he should need to say is she thought that anything was wrong with me, she would have done so this morning, but instead it was good to be complemented, she thinks that I am coping very well, and I agree. I see my errors of the past frightening glimpses of how my behaviour was questionable, this insight was all too familiar especially when mat started to exhibit signs this evening, it was evident, although there have been various other things over the last few weeks; but it is not my responsibility; and he will betaken care of soon enough if anyone feels the need to intervene- close chapter.

Yes Francesca taught me a lot, she was a strong young woman, and gave me strength also to be confident in myself; I searched today for this and was successfully able to regain this strength which to my surprise I haven't lost, it's always been present, just more evident today. She taught me how beauty has many designs, there are many designs of beauty, beauty is unique, and I love to be feminine, especially in the way I dress. This is me. W e were a sisterhood all of our own. She taught me self-respect and how you could be sexy but still reserve your dignity. It was sophisticated to let everyone think that you were a slut and a man-eater, but then at the same time give as good as you got and to always wear the trousers; let them know that you are the boss, this way you remain in control, and as appealing as a damsel can be to men, id they wanted a wife then they wouldn't sleep with a whore. Men respect and secretly love a strong woman, it keeps them on their toes, and you get so much back in return from them as they continually and tirelessly work to keep you happy, it keeps things fresh, cos they always know in the back of their minds how one day you could quite easily walk away with another man, they are not the centre of your universe, and so the best and fulfilling relationships are based on and run like business partnerships where satisfaction at all times is a non compromising result. This prevents boredom cos you and they know that things are never the same old routine all the time everyday, as you satisfy their needs so you make constant demands as a mark of appreciation. I now I certainly tried and experienced sexual antics that I have never wanted to before, and have not repeated since. It's so incredible to feel the power and mutual respect gained from wanting to drink someone's urine, and feel sexually exhilarated, as they beg in return to drink yours. To treat your boyfriend as a homosexual would and stick a bick pen up his arse and have him at the height of pleasure as he also admits it. To dominate and be dominated. To actually ask for a slap in the face and enjoy hitting him first, as he asks you too. But to be punched and actually enjoy it cos this is only how much he loves you. He had trouble expressing himself, and it was only cos he was so worked up, with men it's more physical and then its all over, that's just how his emotions presented themselves. But to actually knee him in the crotch and laugh about it, some may suggest that this is not healthy. But I know that my sexual relationship with him was similar to the sex that Francesca enjoyed, cos we'd talk about it in great detail, she told me how despite her boyfriend loving her they still fought like animals, but she enjoyed the thrill of it, it was exciting and dangerous. I think I was the only person who completely understood her. It ma be suggested that this type of relationship was sick, wrong; but I've come to the firm conclusion that it was just taboo, as we both were willing participants, and as much as we enjoyed the making up and comforting we enjoyed the fights. It was play fights though, even though they were real; it was like sexual freedom on a new level, I have to say that it's an acquired taste. Where a man is a man and a woman a woman, where a woman is not afraid to say I'm your bitch, and a man not afraid to become all possessive and jealous that it turns you both on so much that you have never experienced sex like it- dirty sex and raw. He made me moan so much, he pleasured me to the point of where I could've easily

15

passed out from the height of ecstasy- and to be fulfilling an orgasm where you tell him how this is the closest thing to heaven on earth that you can ever experience, an orgasm, and to mean it in the way that you don't fake it. To whisper sweet nothings and be romantic whilst being dirty, the power of the mind, to the point where he feels like a virgin and is aware of how much he has actually been missing out on, he is uncontrollable he couldn't take his hands off me. We did it and did it and did it again and again. We wrestled playfully seductively amongst the sheets and fell on the floor and laughed hysterically so sure at that point in time that it was the closest anyone could ever get to another human being and feel the same way. He treated me as his mistress and his whore but at the same time his wife and long term girlfriend. Something which is a package you can't get in any relationship. We had the same ideas about sex, and were naturally at ease with each other, we could talk about anything. I have to thank him from saving me from what could've been a rather boring marriage and becoming another Margaret where her husband was sure to have affairs. He brought me back here, he wanted to provide for me, we have an understanding, he doesn't want me to work, and consequently he puts a block on any plans that may progress thus far. He likes to feed me, he loved me as a curvy person, and I know this is true, as he actually wept at the sight of my thin and slimmer body. He couldn't believe how thin I had become, and that it was out of his control. As I told him in Guernsey I was out of his jurisdiction, which is how I know that he has always been pulling strings with various people, and totally exaggerating symptoms. He fears loosing me. And he begged me not to leave him, by this he meant not to marry, as he said that he would kill himself if I ever left him. He said that you are not going to have that dirty old pervert's bastard. He went on to say how he didn't want me to have children. And he wanted to keep me as a little girl. He said how the drugs which sedated me would keep me young as this way he would know where I was in bed resting, he said that when I came back home he would put me back on ice, he said that I had been working too hard, and said that he would beat up my boss for taking advantage of his little girl. I cannot be too hard on him cos when all's said and done I know that he loves me. There's much more to love than the physical side. He told me how despite y thinking of how he shagged around as well as his wife this was not the case, he couldn't bare the thought of being sexual with her of all people as well as others, I believe him cos he unwittingly went to punch me in the face to fend of what he thought was his wife when it was me, he said oh I'm sorry I thought you were her. I know he is largely celibate preferring to wink himself off, and I know that he doesn't want anymore children, he says that he doesn't love his children and that he wishes that I was his. He said I don't care if you think I am old fashioned or a male chauvinist, tough shit cos this is what I am, and you will learn to love me Babes, cos you are mine. This is how I know it is everlasting even to today. We have an old fashioned love, he keeps me like a mistress, and he keeps me at a distance but always I am well cared for, I know he checks that I remain single, he told me that I will keep my legs crossed, and on the odd occasions that you do have sex with other men, this only makes me love you more babes cos I cant wait to come along afterwards and take you off another man again... Oh a nice cigarette beckons as well as the loo, and I realise I love a cigarette cos it draws me close to him, every drag I drag with him...

Well I thought I should write a few thoughts down for good old John. I wonder if he can hear my thoughts being deceased and all that. After another spell in Hospital am feeling more optimistic this time about my recovery. The process takes as long as I need it to you know. And the important thing which I took away from NA was keeping it in the day; or as they say 'Just for today'. Funny thing was that I saw Michael on this occasion, seemed he'd been looking for me, well anyhow I got the word that he was and so arranged to meet him. He was unfaithful to Louise, and for the first time ever he was faithful to me. We connected in more ways than one, and ended up after being thrown out of the Cinema ˋcos they reckoned that I looked too young making Love. He also asked me to marry him, which at first I said no and then I said yes, but this was our thing, which I always did to keep him on his toes. Don't know if anything else will come from this, but at least I know that in his own little way he cares, especially enough to take it to another level, a whole different level whereby it was more than just words and banter some would say harmless enough. I wonder if he knows what happened between his Father and me, I suspect he does. Anyway after all this time he still calls me his baby sister. Its kind of incestuously kinky one of toes things which you'd only understand if you had our kind of relationship. Went to a club Varsity the other night an anyhow I overheard a boy saying to another boy that's the one that Michael`s marrying. I felt so privileged, like he maybe this time he's gonna give me something real, instead of something superficial with holes in and words that have and could have endless meanings and various interpretations. How I agonised over what did he mean when he said that etc, oh so its not over then, maybe in another time and place if I was a size 8 or even pondered how lucky she is to have Michael MY boyfriend all to herself.

Decided to stop my medication and its working have already lost ½ a stone in weight so that's got to be good. Trying to rationalise what to do with this months money, seem to be in need or want of stuff all the time. But I like to pretend that I'm living with Vince (since Michaels not around at the moment- aside I wonder what if I'd got pregnant!) like what if we'd made it, actually were living the dream you know, yes I could hold down a man a real life walking talking man figure, someone not just to make do with but someone that I really loved and fancied to bits; someone like John. I think John would love what I've done with the place. It's all newly decorated, to the point of even getting the ceilings professionally done. New carpets laid some furniture; not everything but it'll come in time. It's going to look like a palace, somewhat of a hotel theme, if not a bed and breakfast upmarket of coarse. New curtains hung. We did all the DIY ourselves, what with drilling. So anyhow John was meaning to talk to you about this month's budget as follows:-

1. Leave I.S and I.C to pay off some of OD.
2. Leaving £300 –Leave Hair this month and instead but a hairdryer from Boots
3. Hairdryer from Boots £20
4. £30 electric
5. Telephone Scottish Power to give gas meter reading to have cheque for credited amount sent out by Bacs even
6. Shopping @£50
7. Leaving a budget of £200 for furniture (i) Coffee table (ii) 2 x Bedside cabinets (iii) Small table and chairs

So I guess that's our list John. Our home is looking like a home now and less like a building site ey. I love you well my hands can't type any longer. Seems easier to speak to you instead the rest of my thoughts, mums' coming in the morning. X

Yes....I think one can safely assume that if he's not coming now- then he never will. And this was indeed the very last chance I gave John.

Well I bet your wondering what the next bit is? I know I certainly was until I managed to summon up the strength and courage to snap out of it. It was almost as though for a number of years I had been in a long and distant trance; and yes admittedly I had been burying my head in the sand not wanting to recognise how distant and apart Mr Zane and I now were. For our final fleeing words to each other were most angry; yet truthful. In a final blazing row.

So what was a girl to do ey? There were hopes and rumours at the total public humiliation and outrage that I would indeed seek residence elsewhere. Mr Zane was kind enough to allow a further 4 years grace on my rented property before I would be forced to vacate. It was a most upsetting time for me; and I cannot begin to describe the hurt and pain that I felt; facing it- we were indeed finally over! It seems Mr Zane did not fully appreciate all my uttermost accomplishments as a woman. And attacking my very looks was the final straw! It would seem that he sought revenge for discovering me and my long term lover Warren. This was indeed the only reason that he took me back – since he just wanted to play one more game that went horribly wrong for all concerned.

It was a time to retreat and regroup with my mum. I always in dire most need would turn to my mum for financial assistance once more. It was only by chance how I had read in the local rag column how I was soon enough to be made homeless. Giving me just enough time to make final preparations to leave. It was a game of intolerable cruelty; since he actually looked me in the eyes and smiled at a most recent meeting which I knew was in my best interests to attend. I could not quite believe how Mr Zane could ever be so devious! All I can do now is to breathe a sigh of relief; for another lucky escape. When considering how at this very moment in time I can look back on this whole horrid business with rose tinted spectacles; since he all along had planned to throw me to the wolves as it were; whilst all the while smiling. I never realised how much he loathed me till now! And now in my later years I was like property something to be discarded with. Sad but true.

Well in the words of my ex boss: he certainly did me a favour – allowing me through publically humiliating me to realise is full rath and scorn. I will never look at him in quite the same way again. But may I say how he greatly underestimated me in terms of my educational background and capabilities. This was the only thing that saved me in essence- from going under- which is what he wanted secretly.

He raged on how he would pursue grounds to put imprison me too (all utter nonsense of course!) – Since he had found out about mine and Warrens` extra-marital affairs – he had indeed been following me for some time- which I was aware of to a point- and not to become overly paranoid. Mr Zane was a cunning man- and not in a good way. We then over the next coming years embarked on what was an ongoing power-struggle. I was a fight – a fight for survival especially with the society in which we both continued to circulate in. Yes a dog-eat dog world! As I said earlier it was very much non-stop revenge antics- in order to continue to punish me for having another man. Who I loved more than him – Mr Zane- and he knew it too! It was not only a fight for survival- but we were both playing for time too. And after exhausting every other avenue for sourcing much needed finance I was able to just in the nick og time go to my mum for assistance. Mum was willing to help me out- but was very much strapped for cash herself and insisted that I repay the monies asap.

What was my next forward steps- well naturally employment. I had to from scratch muster up a home for myself. The jobs market was weak- and I re entered at a crucial time- thank goodness I had the sense to undertake further education studies. And I worked myself every day I returned to work effectively out of poverty.

Mum short term loaned me enough of a small deposit to put on a quite modest but suitable property in another area. Seriously all my accommodation options were in fact exhausted. I worked my fingers to the bone for the first 4 years- as well as completing mandatory levels 2 and 3 diplomas for my place of work. Doing anything for another `career break` as it were. It was hard since the great social life in particular which I had enjoyed was no more. Mr Zane had personally seen to this- in his efforts to run me out of town effectively.

The great city Churches were by this time flooded with gossip as well as sparking outrage. No one was willing to be seen with me publically- it was all very damaging to me particularly. Warren too chose to break off all contact with me- which was tough to bear. The church influence in the city was well liked and respected- even if a little backward and judgemental- which was why my illegitimates were since removed. They argued it was for the greater good of society- and this sort of thing should not be seen- least of all if it does go on. They argued not in our church! Social hypocrites that they were. For so long as one followed the rules then they had great future promises for their families- and their families alone. This to me questioned liberty itself- since it impacted on freedom of choice- sexual partnering especially. I know my ex by now as coming to be know – Mr Zane had time to talk to Warren. He couldn't help himself- and attacked the very nature of our love-making itself. He basically warned him off!

As time went on it became increasingly difficult to make new friends as well as form new attachments- the very stench of our breakup was everywhere! Mr Zane was a well liked man- and I was now nothing more than a cheap slut!

People would indeed cross the street at my very presence- and refuse to talk and say hello. It would seem that everywhere I went I was to be shunned.

Those individuals were did speak to me were most unpleasant too- it was like ex-boyfriends united- each taking cheap shots. Because lets face it nobody really likes their ex!? All I will say is how the matter increasingly got more and more out of hand to the point whereby I needed the assistance of the police on a regular basis. What also became more apparent was how if it wasn't one ex making problems it was another! Anyway it was hard to keep track of. As one insignificant even thought to himself – great now's my chance to get back with me?! It was no laughing matter.

I to mainly console myself as well as to save my own sanity would constantly be defining myself- and I nowadays found that I would be committed to stating how I was a single independent woman! This was just to avoid any further rumours or confusion. As by now I had resorted myself to draw a line under all of the above ex boyfriends over the years and instead focus on myself. But not ready to accept that there was indeed anything wrong with me. Because I had to stop beating myself up.

I know I was the better person for always seeking self-improvement. And Warren who I so dearly loved was no longer warren any more! My worst fears had been confirmed- confined to drug-addiction- I lost him in the battle. He had turned to drugs and there was no way I could get him back now. I was simply too late. For all he craved now was his next fix- I despaired over and over. His once fine figure of a man was now reduced greatly. There was no way I could help him- because he didn't want to be helped any more. Yes I believe he was indeed targeted because of his involvement with me; and now instead of running away together he was in the grips of drug addiction. There was just no way out. What was just as bad was how he now hated me too. I know his friends and family blamed me too for his downfall.

For some time I carried on with a little hope and optimism that he would return to me- and my new property would provide some sort of safe haven for him and I. If only I could reach him. I was soooo angry as well as saddened- part of me wanted to give him a good shake- and part of me wanting to look after him- and bring him back somehow. His friend shared no sympathy with me- and eventually became pulled in to combing the streets for him- along with me. Hours and hours I walked those streets- has any body seen him? Fuck knows where he was- or who he as with- since these professed to be his knew friends now!? God knows what rubbish they were filling his fragile head with!

My prayers have been answered; after being on the point of giving up on Warren- then one day he eventually came to me. I'll never forget it…..he actually said that he loves me! Whilst I remain celibate at this time. And have done so for a long while now – not only out of self-respect but because this time it's serious! Every so often I keep being asked as well if I have a boyfriend currently. Everyone is so intrigued to know! I continue to wear a ring of sorts on my wedding finger as a silent token of my commitment to the 'one'! Out of my modest jewellery collection much of which was sold off effectively in order to settle debts- and basically to feed me.

What can I say it actually happened – the earth moved for both of us- and seriously we only needed one chance/opportunity in order for Warren to effectively impregnate me. It's what we both wanted – believe me I actually checked this at the time of intercourse....hahahaha because it was important to me. The sex was great. And now secretly his love-child grows inside me. It's a good feeling to have to feel the baby move from time to time; I continue to look after myself in ensuring that I have enough to eat and drink whilst re-educating myself in relation to being nutritionally aware. I already have made room in my property to accommodate the baby. It's such a nice sized room too – and all that I can afford currently based on my income. In fact it was only the other day that I hung the curtains in this room- to complete the look as it were- and they are the same curtains which I bought from the original first home. I'm sooo pleased to have moved now to this new home since I am able to start afresh whist the old place now holds too many bad memories of Mr Zane for instance.

I'm soo in love with Warren- all I can think of now is supporting our dysfunctional family i.e. the life growing inside me. I've come a long way from the old council estate and needed to retrain in my job role. I think that I am mentally planning our babys` first Xmas and all the toys that I shall buy- the music, the dancing etc- and even mum coming round and celebrating our time together.

There was one massive secret which I continued to harbour though – and it all surrounded Warren- in a deeply personal way. For whilst it preceeded that Warren and I only made love on one occasion- it was sooo special- for it would appear that Warren was indeed a virgin! – it was sooo special for us both- the intimate details were forever etched on my brain- for it was not until we got down to it- that we found out together and discovered the truth! It was so intense- especially the way he held me in his arms- for I shall never forget it! The way he kissed me too- yes he was indeed a virgin. Every so often I will just have to take stock of this moment- and you may catch me- in a sort of wandersome gaze- this is usually the time when I'm thinking about it- and reliving it over and over again! It is also a special time that when I am on my own I will think about this. In fact after I had this great sexual experience with Warren I never went/or cared to go with another man again.

My friendship circles were very strained at this time. Mr Zane knew it too; for it would seem that my incredible beauty and overwhelming influence would soon rival his. I knew Mr Zane would continue to cause me difficulties at large in the community. He had an apt way of using people effectively. This was in fact how I still consider our relationship- in as much as I needed him – it turned out that he needed me too. I think you never realise how wicked a person is 'till you end things with them I suppose. Mr Zane was very envious of my social circles- and I knew through utilising gutter people (for want of a better word) he then proceeded to put the `boot in` and proceed to ruin my reputation. Since it especially emerged that I had Royal connections too. Mr Zane and his feeble attempts to try to ultimately control and co-erce me was now over. Whilst he argued with me that he had rather a lot of money; I just feel that given my own life-experience how his play-boy days were now his downfall- indeed with my good self. I think if anything I learnt this was in fact that no matter how much money an individual has, sooner or later one has to address the finer points in life like being an accomplished individual. It was a very trying time for me since no way was I going to become hooked on drugs or alcohol- for this reason Mr Zane insisted that I was a bore! And because of my many female friendships this made me a lesbian- I don't think so Mr Zane. In addition the reason I had a sperm donor was because I was ugly?! Mr Zane you are a nightmare. In fact I know that if not himself he took the liberty of contacting various friends to have a word as it were. I know the orders came from high up- and through these ill-sexual politics which I refuse to become involved in these days basically these men were safeguarding their jobs. Professionally I once more became a formidable force and I know that I threaten him as a woman in my own right. I became headhunted for my amazing professional capabilities- and playing sexual politics was indeed just another way to destroy me ultimately.

I will argue how Mr Zane became obsessed and it greatly angered him the degree of my intelligence. So for all intents and purposes- and as I was looking for a greater calibre of man-material I served to continue with educational studies. Mr Zane was a great bother to me- even publically embarrassing me- as well as threatening to put my close friends in prison; knowing that full well- some of my friends did not have the financial means to fight him off effectively. Another example of an abuse of power- Mr Zane was in fact of the school of do as I say or else I will ruin you!

Mr Zane was in fact a very dangerous man to become deeply involved with. And to this day if anyone asks me about Mr Zane I simply tell them that he is a lovely man. Since there are those who he is more kind towards than others for a while- or at least `til they have served their purpose for him that is. I will always say that the next few years onwards became a bit of a cat and mousse struggle for me. It was Mr Zane laughing at me - `...see I've got you there sweetheart...`!

If it was not for my strong connections too I would have gone under. My level head saved me a great deal. I know Mr Zane would sometimes venture down and pay local hit-men as it was- gutter people with not much to loose- it was once suggested to me then that they were sticking it to the man- since they would happily attack the rich or anyone perceived to have money – in order to bring them down effectively. I know it was an inside job- he put people up to this too. No one dared to speak out against him either or to challenge him. Naturally Mr Zane needed/required a good deal of support. I was very thankful that he never got to the bottom of all of my entire friendship groups- for this was indeed my escape plan/route. For I knew the bastard would betray me for a few pieces of silver. As one day I suggested to him that quite simply- he had no loyalty towards me. It came as no surprise that he wanted to cut my throat effectively. Given past experiences whereby old boyfriends have double-crossed me- I only trust certain people- and always make contingency plans way ahead of time..... in order for when the weeding process begins and times become a little harder. Currently just to comment on the economic climate being such that we are in a recession.

After much in the way of trials and tribulations with ongoing neighbourhood struggles etc. It finally hit me like a tonne of bricks- basically this Warren had indeed helped me tremendously in getting over Mr Zane. He'd also gone onto provide me with a ready-made family (if you'll take my point)....I knew that the most precious gift he could give me.....as an added symbol of our love eternal was indeed our lovechild. Certainly; he joked not when he said to me how he never wanted me to be on my own. I came to accept how he would never actually be with me on a more permanent basis- however when we came together on that night to make love essentially- in my life certainly it would prove to change everything forever- as a token of our deep and lasting affections for each other. Would we ever need to say anything more than this? For the baby just alone serves to speak volumes; as I always maintained how `truth` is a funny old phenomenon – I accepted his illegitimate baby naturally. However this continued to spark much outrage from certain corners.

I have never been so happy in all my life to be finally expecting his lovechild. Pity it couldn't be said of other parties. Let it be known that I fought in vain for every love-child that I went on to be pregnant with.....but I never gave up hope that I shall be re-united with my children especially after all my continued efforts. I took a vow of chastity and remained celibate for quite a considerable length of time. Warren became such a fix-me all –up tonic- and to this day remains the love of my life. Unfortunately for Mr Zane I never forgave him. But better to find out sooner than later. For he had indeed rumbled our long-term affair. All I ever wanted was a baby/child of my own – like most women of a certain age do- a natural instinct. And at last I am happy- for how dare anyone think that they have the right to deny me my happiness? These days I refuse to have anyone making decisions on my behalf for me. Let anyone else fall victim to the backwards mental health system- so many years of my life I had been effectively robbed of. As it begun to sink in that I did not want any of my ex boyfriends back- they just grew more and more nastier towards me- especially after discovering how I had met Warren and now bearing his love-child was building a better life for myself. I even had to report some unwanted male/s for stalking me effectively- I made my feelings plain; I didn't want another man aside from Warren. Warren and I are very much real people with real lives. Society is not perfect these days... but we made the best of what there was between us.